Laurie Foos

TOAST

Laurie Foos is the author of *Ex Utero*, *Portrait of the Walrus by a Young Artist*, *Twinship*, *Before Elvis There was Nothing*, *The Blue Girl*, and *Bingo Under the Crucifix*. Her non-fiction has appeared in *Brain, Child* and in the anthology *So Glad They Told Me: Women Get Real about Motherhood*. She teaches in the Bachelor of Fine Arts Program at Goddard College and in the Master of Fine Arts Program at Lesley University.

Laurie's first book in the series was *The Giant Baby*.

First published by GemmaMedia in 2018.

GemmaMedia
230 Commercial Street
Boston MA 02109 USA

www.gemmamedia.com

©2018 by Laurie Foos

Printed in the United States of America
978-1-936846-67-2

Library of Congress Cataloging-in-Publication Data

Foos, Laurie, 1966– author.
Toast / Laurie Foos.
Boston, MA : GemmaMedia, 2018. | Series: Gemma open door
LCCN 2018036517 | ISBN 9781936846672
LCC PS3556.O564 T63 2018 | DDC 813/.54--dc23
LC record available at https://lccn.loc.gov/2018036517

Cover by Laura Shaw Design

Gemma's Open Doors provide fresh stories, new ideas, and essential resources for young people and adults as they embrace the power of reading and the written word.

Brian Bouldrey
Series Editor

GEMMA

Open Door

For Ella and Zachariah

CHAPTER 1

Will is watching videos on his iPad when I come downstairs. When I sit down next to him at the kitchen table, he doesn't look up at me. I look over at the wall where Mom has pinned what she calls the "visual schedule" she's made for Will on the corkboard on the wall. My stomach squeezes a little.

Today is a big day in our house. Today we're getting a babysitter, and not just a babysitter who comes after school and lets you Google the answers for your math homework. Not one who sits on the couch texting her boyfriend while you watch a movie your parents won't let you see. Today we're getting a babysitter who is going to stay with us while Mom and Dad go away overnight.

This is totally unheard of in our house. We have not had a babysitter, ever, in the history of my being alive who wasn't Gram. Also, my parents have never gone overnight anywhere that I can remember. Sometimes we'd stay at Gram's house. But when we went to Gram's, Mom and Dad always stayed home. Gram died two years ago, when I was nine and Will was eight.

Dad sets Will's toast on a paper plate. Will picks the toast up and examines it.

Will's toast has to be more tan than brown because if it's too brown, there's no way Will is going to eat it.

"How is it, buddy?" Dad asks. "Is it tan enough? Not too brown?"

Will puts the toast back down on the plate and hands the plate to Dad.

"There's not enough tan," Will says. "It's burnt."

I look at the toast. It is browner than the toast that Mom makes. But it's definitely not burnt.

"I want Mom to make my toast," Will says.

Dad throws the toast in the garbage and starts again.

"Mom is packing," Dad says. "I'm making the toast today."

I want to ask Dad if he's explained about the toast to the babysitter, if she knows all the things Will doesn't like. I don't get the chance, though, because

Dad is suddenly standing over me at the table and smiling. He hands me my plate of toast. He doesn't ask me if mine is the right color.

"Well, it's a banner day in the Hamilton house," Dad says to me and winks. "Isn't that right, Mia?"

The visual schedule has times and pictures of things that Will does. It helps him when things change. On the paper Mom has printed out is a picture of the babysitter. She has red curly hair and wears a light blue T-shirt with the words "Be Kind" on it. In big letters it says "Shelby," and then underneath it says "Babysitter."

I push my toast around my plate and smile at Dad because I know he wants me to smile. I'm pretty good at knowing what other people want. Mom says I have a lot of empathy, which is a fancy way of saying that I understand what other people are feeling. It's also what makes me such a great big sister, she says.

When Dad hands Will his new slices of toast, Will picks the toast up and holds it in front of his face.

"Come on, Will," I say. "That toast is definitely tan."

He nods and takes a bite.

"Yup," he says, "definitely tan."

Dad gives me a thumbs-up and says he's going to take a shower. My toast is cold. I eat it anyway.

Will looks up from his iPad and

starts looking around the room and up at the ceiling.

"Where is it?" Will says. "Where did Dad put it?"

For a minute I don't know what he means.

"Where did Dad put what?" I say.

"I don't see it," Will says. "The banner."

There are toast crumbs all over Will's iPad. Usually that grosses me out, but not today. Today I know what I have to do once that babysitter gets here. Today I have to be what Mom says I am: a good big sister.

Will has what Mom calls "a literal mind."

"Oh," I say. "There's no real banner. It's just an expression."

Will wipes his mouth on the collar of his shirt and goes back to looking at his iPad.

"It's just an expression," he says.

CHAPTER 2

Last week at the bus stop I thought about telling my friend Hannah about the babysitter. Then I remembered that Hannah has a different babysitter every time I'm over there. Since we met in fourth grade, she must have had around twenty of them. For some reason they all have long dark hair and wear gray hoodies. Once when I asked Hannah if she ever noticed that, she said sometimes she wonders if her parents rent babysitters from some company. I imagined all these babysitters with dark hair and hoodies lined up on a conveyor belt. I wondered what would happen if the conveyor belt pushed its way to our door instead. It's not that I was jealous, but I wondered. Hannah said the babysitters let her stay up late and drink soda. Some of them even let her curse.

Now that we're actually getting one, though, I'm not wondering so much. Instead I have this little squeezing feeling in my stomach. There will be someone staying with us who won't know all the things that Will likes and doesn't like. Someone who won't know all the important things there are to know about Will.

I go into Mom's room and sit on her bed while she packs. There are at least four pairs of jeans laid out on the bed. It looks like she dumped her whole underwear drawer on there, too.

I'd rather not look at Mom's underwear, so I scoot up by the pillows.

"Mom," I say, "what if Will doesn't
listen to the babysitter when you're
gone?"

Mom looks at me as she folds and
refolds a black sweater before putting
it into the suitcase that already looks
too full.

"Shelby," she says. "Her name is
Shelby. And he will. He'll listen."

I pick up one of her pairs of socks
and squeeze it.

"What if he throws things in his
room again while you're gone?"

Mom sighs a little and holds one of
Dad's T-shirts in her hands.

"She's studying to be a Special Ed

teacher," Mom says. "I told you this already. Remember?"

I lie back on the pillow and press my face against the comforter. I squeeze the ball of socks and think about what she told me about this babysitter, Shelby, when she first brought up the idea.

She puts Dad's T-shirt in the suitcase and looks at me. She tells me again that the babysitter is not a stranger, that she's the daughter of some old friend of the family. We did meet her, but I had a social studies test the next day and wasn't paying much attention. I remember she had long red hair. Will stayed on his iPad the whole time watching videos. When

Mom asked if it was okay with Will if Shelby came to babysit one day, Will didn't look up from the iPad.

"Will," Mom had said, "can you look at Mommy?"

He looked up and blinked.

"Is it okay if Shelby comes to baby-sit you and Mia next week?"

Will lifted the collar of his shirt into his mouth and chewed on it a few times. I remember I wished he would stop eating his shirt and went back to studying for social studies.

"Yup, it's okay," Will said. "Yup."

Will always says "yup," "never," "yeah," or "yes." It's just one of the things he does.

"Shelby is an aide in a classroom for kids on the spectrum," Mom tells me. She shoves more shirts into the suitcase. "She knows all about Will."

There's something about those words that I don't like. *On the spectrum.* They always make me think of some cheesy rainbow drawing full of yellows and purples and reds. I don't like anything that's cheesy. It's not like I love the word *autism*, either. If I had to pick between the two, though, I guess I would choose the word autism.

"Okay," I say, "but what if . . .?"

Mom doesn't let me finish and sits down on the bed next to me.

"Mia," she says, "you have to stop with all the 'what-ifs.' That's what moms are for, right?"

I say, "Right," but I don't stop, not really.

"Look, honey," she says with her hand on my leg, "I'm a little nervous, too. We're only going ten minutes away. It's going to be fine."

I want to know why they have to bother going at all if they're only going ten minutes away, but I don't say this to Mom.

Instead I just say, "I'm not nervous." Then I leave her there to deal with all of her underwear and socks and the millions of other things she's stuffing into her suitcase.

What if Shelby doesn't know that Will needs to line up his stuffed animals on his dresser before he goes to bed? What if she doesn't know how to make his frozen pizza, that it has to be just the right amount of crispy? What if she doesn't know what he means when he says things from TV and movies and the iPad? What then?

CHAPTER 3

I decide to play *Minecraft* with Will while
we wait for the babysitter—Shelby—to
get here. Will loves *Minecraft*. Before
Minecraft he played *Super Mario*, and
before *Super Mario* he only played with
Thomas the Tank Engine. He used to
build tracks all over the house. Some
of his tracks would reach all the way
across the living room rug, then go up
one side of the couch, across the top,
then back down to the rug again. With
his tracks all over the place, we couldn't
watch TV in there or sit on either of the
couches. Mom would take pictures of
the tracks before she vacuumed so she
could remember how to put them back
together just the way he left them. If she

put them back the wrong way or forgot a piece, Will would freak.

Mom doesn't say "freak." She says "meltdown."

One day I heard Will ask Mom if Thomas the Tank Engine was for babies.

"Thomas isn't for babies," she said. "You love Thomas. Are you a baby?"

I didn't know any boys who still wore Thomas shirts to school. Usually I don't pay much attention to what other people wear. I knew none of the boys in my class had worn Thomas shirts since around first grade. Maybe even since kindergarten. So, I decided to tell Will myself. I went into his room after Mom tucked him in, and I told him.

"Will," I said, "Remember what you asked Mom about Thomas?"

He was lying in his bed with his Thomas blanket and Thomas pillowcase and Thomas stickers on the walls. I knew Mom would never tell him the truth. Someone had to.

"It's true," I whispered to him. "Thomas is for babies."

"Thomas is for babies?" he said.

"Yup," I said.

I kind of expected he might start crying and run and tell Mom. Instead he just turned over and faced the wall. Really quietly he said, "Thomas is for babies. Thomas is for babies."

"Right," I said.

The next day he took apart the tracks from all over the couches. He didn't freak out, not even once. When Dad asked where he wanted to put all his trains and tracks, he said, "Down in the basement. Thomas is for babies."

Later Dad stopped me outside my room and put his hand on my shoulder.

"Tell me the truth," Dad said. "Did you tell him that? That Thomas is for babies?"

For a minute I wondered if Dad would be mad at me. Then I remembered what I'd heard Mom say once on the phone to one of her friends. "The problem is," she said, "that Will wouldn't even know if he was being made fun of."

"Dad," I said, "I was just looking out for him."

He gave me a little squeeze and

said that he'd thought of telling Will that himself but was too afraid of Mom to do it. Then we both laughed and gave each other a high five.

Mom once said it made her a little sad that Will had to say goodbye to Thomas. Now, Will plays *Super Mario* again, but *Minecraft* is his favorite. He wears *Minecraft* shirts and has a *Minecraft* wallet and a *Minecraft* poster in his room. One thing about Will— when he gets into something, he gets totally into it.

Last year Hannah and I would play *Minecraft* and talk about it sometimes at lunch. This year we don't talk about it anymore. I don't know for sure whether Hannah gave up playing, but she never mentions it. So, I just play with Will.

I'm planting crops and trying to keep Will from blowing up my village when the doorbell rings. Dad says he'll get it while Mom stands looking at the visual schedule on the wall with pictures of Will and his just-the-right-shade-of-tan toast and his frozen pizza and his iPad. She plays with her fingernails, looks over at Will and then at me. I can hear Dad laughing in the other room. When I look back at the screen, Will has set off bombs in all my crops.

Just then Dad comes into the room with the babysitter. She shakes Mom's hand. Her curly red hair bounces a little when she pumps Mom's hand up and down. Mom looks over her shoulder at me. My crops are destroyed.

"Mia, you remember Shelby, right?" Mom says.

Her voice sounds too high when she says it and cracks a little at the end. Her eyes have that watery look that they get sometimes when Will's bus driver changes and he jumps up and down screaming because he doesn't like change. That happened on the first day of school this year, even though Mom made what's called a social story with pictures of a bus and a driver. I know Mom thinks of me as somebody with lots of empathy, someone who is always a great big sister to Will. That day that he jumped up and down screaming in the driveway, I saw the kid across the street staring at Will. She's younger than us with a long blond ponytail and a mother who never waves back at Mom. That day part of me wanted to yell out, "What are you looking at?" while Will screamed and jumped and flapped his hands around. Sometimes when those things happen I can't help but go someplace far inside myself.

When Shelby says hi, I realize that I must have done that the day she came over to meet us because I can't remember much about that day. I say hi to Shelby and try to plant some new crops.

"Will," Mom says, "can you say hi to Shelby?"

Will mutters "hi" and bombs more of my crops. I just let him.

"Will," Mom says again, "can you look at Shelby when you say hi?"

He looks up really fast and says, "Hi, Shelby," then looks right back at the screen.

"Hey, Will," Shelby says. "You guys like *Minecraft*, huh?"

She sits down between Will and me at the kitchen table. I look up at Mom and Dad. They're standing by the refrigerator, whispering to each other. When Dad sees me looking, he gives me a thumbs-up. I think this is super cheesy, but I keep it to myself.

"I like *Minecraft*, too," Shelby says. "Maybe we all can play later. How does that sound?"

Shelby looks at me and smiles with a lot of teeth. She pushes some of her red hair back behind her ear. She is not wearing a hoodie.

"Does that sound okay, Mia?" she says.

I think about all the babysitters Hannah has had with their long dark hair and their hoodies. I think about the conveyor belt coming out of the imaginary babysitter factory and realize maybe I'm glad it never stopped at our door.

I'm about to tell Shelby "yes" because I know it's rude not to answer. Before I can say anything, though, Will says, really loudly, "You are a toy!"

Mom and Dad stop whispering in

the corner. Shelby looks a little surprised and raises her eyebrows, which are red, just like her hair.

"What was that, Will?" Shelby says, and Will says back, "You are made of plastic. You are a child's plaything."

Mom and Dad don't laugh, but I do. I can tell they're trying to figure out whether Shelby knows what's going on. I know right away it's from *Toy Story*. It's from the part where Woody first meets Buzz Lightyear. Buzz doesn't realize he is only a toy.

"That's from *Toy Story*," I say.

Dad tells Shelby that if she doesn't understand anything Will says, she should just ask me. They say I'm his interpreter.

"Anything you don't understand," Dad says, "Mia will translate."

Sometimes they ask me how I always know what Will means when he says things that are random. I don't know how I do, really. I just do.

CHAPTER 4

By the time Mom and Dad leave, Mom has hugged me and Will around ten thousand times and goes over everything on the visual schedule another million. Shelby tells Mom that she promises she'll call if there are any problems. I feel a little sorry for Mom, who looks like she might cry. Dad puts his arm around her waist and gets her to walk to the front door.

Mom squeezes me one last time and presses her mouth to my ear.

"Everything is going to be fine," Mom says, and I nod and hug her back. I'm not sure if she's saying it for me or for herself. Also I can't figure out why Mom hired Shelby in the first place when it seems like she doesn't really want to go.

"Be a good boy, Will," Mom calls, and I hear Will just say, "Yup."

Now she really does have tears in her eyes. Before she can start crying, Dad practically drags her out to the car. Shelby stands next to me by the front door. We wave to Mom, who is waving with her hand moving up and down as fast as it will go. I wave back and try to stop myself from letting some more *what-ifs* creep into my thoughts. Finally, when the car is out of sight, Shelby closes the door and looks at me.

Now, what? I think.

"So," Shelby says, "should we play some *Minecraft*?"

I don't tell Shelby that Will has never played *Minecraft* with anyone but me. I don't say that Will's friends from school never come over here. I don't say that's because the last time Will had a friend over from school, he went up to his room and threw things because he didn't want to share. Instead I just say, "Sure."

CHAPTER 5

Shelby is terrible at *Minecraft*. She does seem to know how to play, though, and she's not too bad at building. She can't figure out how to get away from the creepers or the villagers. As soon as she finishes building her house, Will blows it up. I think maybe we should have played in Creative Mode so Will couldn't blow anything up. You can only do that in Survival Mode. But Shelby doesn't seem to mind.

After a while Shelby looks up at the clock and says, "Oh, look at that, you guys. It's almost time for lunch."

She closes her laptop and goes over to the wall to take down the visual schedule Mom made. I close my laptop too, because by now I'm hungry and getting tired of playing. I don't think Will gets tired of *Minecraft*, ever. He even dreams about *Minecraft*. Once when we were both sick and slept in Mom's bed, Will said, "Watch out for that creeper," in his sleep. He even dreams about *Minecraft*.

I go to the refrigerator and take out my yogurt. If Mom and Dad were here, I'd probably sit there until one of them got it for me. It doesn't feel right to have Shelby do it, so I get it myself.

On the visual schedule Mom made, there's a picture of Will's frozen pizza box with another picture of the pizza after it came out of the toaster oven. Underneath the paper plate, it says, *Time For Pizza*, and then *Crispy, But Not Too Crispy*.

Shelby takes down the visual schedule and brings it over to Will.

"Look Will," she says, and points. "It says here it's time for pizza."

Will doesn't answer. I shove a spoonful of yogurt in my mouth.

"That means that you'll have to stop playing *Minecraft* soon, right?"

Will looks up at me and the back at the screen.

"Yup," he says.

Shelby slides the pizza into the toaster oven and waits. Will doesn't stop playing.

Once when Dad kept telling Will to stop playing and get off his laptop,

Will just wouldn't listen. We were going to the movies that day, and even though Will likes going to the movies, he refused to stop playing that day. Finally, Dad said that we had to go *now, right now*, and closed the lid of the laptop. Hard. Will ran upstairs and started screaming and crying, "Am I grounded? Am I grounded?" We never got to the movies that day. At lunch Hannah and all the girls at our table would talk about the movie, and I'd pretend that I'd seen it too. I had to wait for it to come out on DVD, which felt like forever.

The beeper on the toaster oven goes off. Will says, "My pizza's done," but he doesn't stop playing.

Shelby gets the pizza out of the toaster oven. She puts the pizza down on a plate next to Will and waits.

"Will," she says, "time to turn off the game and eat your lunch."

Will doesn't look up.

"I want Mom to make my pizza," he says.

I get that squeezing feeling in my stomach again and eat my yogurt as fast as I can.

"Mom isn't here," Shelby says. "Remember? I'm taking care of you today."

Will looks over at me.

"I want Mom to make my pizza," he says again. "Mimi, I want Mom to make my pizza."

Only two people have ever called me Mimi: Gram and Will. I don't let anyone else call me that. Ever.

"Mom went to a hotel with Dad," I say. "You said goodbye to them. You waved."

He blinks a few times.

"I waved," he says. "Yup. I waved goodbye to Mom."

Sometimes Will has what Mom calls "delayed reactions" to things. What might upset other people right away takes Will a lot longer. When Gram died, Will didn't get upset or act like he missed Gram. Then, about three weeks later, he cried every night and couldn't sleep.

"Your pizza is going to get cold," I

say. "You don't like it when your pizza gets cold."

He nods and says, "My pizza is gonna get cold. Yup."

Then just like that, he closes the laptop and starts eating.

"Mama mia," he says after a couple of bites. "Let's-a-go."

I finish the last spoonful of my yogurt and get up to throw it away.

"That's from *Super Mario*," I say, "but it means he likes it."

Shelby smiles at me then.

"How do you know everything he says?" she asks.

I just shrug. I don't know how I do, really. I just do.

CHAPTER 6

Mom calls not long after lunch is over. Will is eating one of his mini bags of Doritos and watching his iPad again. I hear Shelby saying that everything's fine, that Will ate all his pizza. Yes, she says, it was crunchy enough. She tells Mom that I ate all the yogurt, yes, all the way down to the bottom. I make a face because I can't help it. Sometimes Mom thinks I'm still three. Shelby catches me and smiles, then says that Mom wants to say hi.

I take the phone into the living room and look out the window. It's strange to see Shelby's little blue car and not ours in the driveway.

"Everything's going okay?" Mom says. "Shelby's nice, right?"

I tell her yes because I guess it's true. Shelby seems nice.

She asks again if Will ate his pizza and whether I finished my yogurt. I'm not sure why she asks when Shelby just told her, but I tell her anyway. I try to remember if I ever got this squeezing feeling in my stomach when Gram stayed with us when she was still here. That seems so long ago now that I can't remember.

"If there are any problems at all, if Will . . .," she says. But then she stops. "Shelby knows where we are," she says. "The number is on the fridge."

I already know this. I tell myself

to ask Hannah when we go back to school on Monday if her mother shows her phone numbers and asks the same questions a million times. But I already know the answer.

Then Mom asks if she can say hi to Will. I don't know why she asks because Will isn't very good with the phone. When Gram would call, he would yell, "9-1-1, 9-1-1, what is your emergency?" into the phone until Mom or Dad took the phone away from him.

I bring the phone over to Will and tell him Mom wants to say hi. His mouth is orange from the Doritos. Shelby goes to hand him a napkin. He wipes it on his shirt instead.

"Come on, Will," I say. "Mom wants to say hi."

"I want Mom to make my pizza," he says.

"You just ate," I say, and tap my finger on the phone. "She's on the phone. She can't make your pizza."

When I press the receiver to his ear, Will says, "You can't make my pizza," and then he yells out, "If you can't say somethin' nice, don't say nothin' at all!"

After I hang up, I say to Shelby, "That's from *Bambi*."

I try to remember the last time we saw *Bambi* because it's not a movie we usually watch. Then I remember that we used to watch that at Gram's.

*   *   *   *   *

After Shelby cleans up the table, Will goes into the living room to do what Dad calls his "marching routine." Usually I don't pay that much attention to what Will does, but with Shelby here, I notice things more. Sometimes that happens when we're out at a store or when Mom would pick us up last year when we still went to the same school. One day Mom was standing there talking to the lady at the greeter's desk while Will was busy chewing on the sleeve of his sweatshirt. I saw this kid looking at Will—I think he was a third grader—and making a face. I pulled Will's arm down and told him to stop. I couldn't wait to get out of there. In the car on the way home, I couldn't stop noticing that the sleeve of Will's hoodie was soaked. If it's just the four of us, though, I don't care how much Will chews on his sleeves.

Will marches from one end of the living room to the other. He does this over and over again. He makes his arms stiff like a soldier when he walks. When he gets to the part where he has to turn around, he stops and says to himself, "I like *Minecraft*." He says that three times. Then he marches the other way.

Shelby comes over to where I'm standing and watching Will and shows me the visual schedule.

"After lunch, your mom wrote "Free Time," she says. She looks over

at Will marching but doesn't say anything. "What do you guys usually do
after lunch?"

I watch Will marching back and
forth, back and forth. I wonder if
Will's marching routine counts as part
of free time. It's definitely something
he does on the weekends. Sometimes
Mom takes him to something called
a sensory gym, which is a place with
ball pits and beanbag chairs and tram-
polines. But I don't think that's one of
the choices.

I just shrug. For some reason
watching Will do the marching routine with Shelby there gives me that
squeezing feeling in my stomach
again.

"I don't know why he does that," I say, "in case you were wondering."

Shelby smiles with her head tilted a little.

"Actually, I wasn't wondering," she says.

She tells me that some of the kids in her classroom do things like that too. It's the first time she's mentioned her classroom. I want to go ask her what kinds of things, but I don't.

"Why don't we go outside for a while?" she says. "It's really nice out."

I'm about to tell her that sometimes it's hard to get Will to stop marching, but I don't get a chance. She tells Will she's going to set the timer on her phone for four minutes.

When the timer goes off, she says Will has to stop marching.

"Okay, Will?" she says, and Will just says, "Yup."

When the timer goes off, Will runs for the back door and yells back at us, "So long, boys!"

Shelby laughs a little, and I do too. I know that line is from the movie *Up*, but since she doesn't ask, I don't say anything. I keep it to myself.

CHAPTER 7

Outside we kick the ball around the yard for a while. I find the ball in the shed next to the lawn mower, one of Will's old Thomas balls. We stand in a triangle. Shelby stands by the apple tree, Will stands by the patio, and I stand by the shed. Shelby says she'll kick the ball to Will, then Will should kick it to me. Then I should kick it back to Shelby. And so on. Easy. But not for Will. Twice she kicks it to Will, and he kicks it right back to her.

"That's okay," Shelby says, stopping the Thomas ball with her foot. "This time kick it to Mia."

When the ball comes for him, he

misses. Then he kicks it back to Shelby again.

"No, Will," I say, because I'm getting tired of standing there. "Kick it to me this time. Not Shelby."

Will yells out, "Don't run in the hallway!" and kicks it back to Shelby again.

I try not to laugh. Last year he kept saying, "You can't go on the computer if you don't stop crying." Mom got really mad when she heard that one. I heard her telling Dad that she knew one of the aides in the class must have said that to him. "You know that's his echolalia," Mom said. "That's something that was said to him that he repeated. Will doesn't make things up."

It's true that Will doesn't make

things up. He also doesn't lie. I don't think he can.

"Kick it to Shelby," I say again.

When the ball rolls up to his foot, he kicks it really hard. It goes way over Shelby's head and lands in the tree. I can see the red ball with Thomas's blue face all the way up in one of the highest branches.

"Oh, no! Oh, no!" he says. He puts his hands over his ears. "Mimi's going to get mad at me! Mimi's going to get really mad!"

He keeps his hands over his ears and says it again.

"It's all right, Will," Shelby says. "Mia's not mad."

I'm glad she didn't call me Mimi.

"Are you mad, Mia?" she says.

Whenever Will does something, even by accident, he thinks people are mad at him. I don't know why. Once Mom said, "There are things Will just doesn't understand. And maybe won't, ever." She said this when Will overflowed the toilet the day after Gram died. He flushed some of his play sand down the bowl. Dad yelled at him that day to never, ever throw anything down the toilet again. For about a week afterward, he kept saying, "Dad is really mad at me. Why is Dad so mad?"

I know he doesn't understand some things. Sometimes I try to imagine what it would be like to not understand. But I just can't. Maybe I don't have so much empathy after all.

"I'm not mad," I say, even though we have to end the game.

When I was little, I used to think that Will went someplace called "Spectrum School." Will was in preschool then, and I was in Kindergarten. Every day Gram would get me off the bus while Mom went to pick him up. After school these two ladies would come to the house to do puzzles and play with Play-Doh with Will at the kitchen table. Sometimes I'd play too, when I was finished with my homework. One day I asked Mom how much longer he had to go to Spectrum School, and Mom and the ladies laughed and laughed.

I still don't know why this was so funny to them.

Sometimes Will would throw the Play-Doh on the floor. Sometimes he ate it. When that happened, the lady would close up the cans and put them away. Sometimes he threw the puzzle pieces on the floor and started screaming. Once he smacked the lady when she took the Play-Doh away. When I laughed, Mom shushed me and sent me to my room to color.

Later, after we play Go Fish—every time someone has to go fish, Will sings, "Just keep swimming, just keep swimming" from *Finding Dory*—Shelby says she has a surprise for us. She says that Mom said we could have this surprise if we had a great day.

"I'd say this has been a great day, wouldn't you?" Shelby asks.

She has her hands on her hips. Her red hair bounces when she reaches for her cell phone on the table. Will and I play *Minecraft* again. This time I set it to Creative Mode so Will can't blow anything up. I don't know if this has been a great day, but it hasn't been a disaster either.

I can see Shelby from the doorway walking back toward the kitchen with the phone to her ear. I just know Mom is going to want to talk to me again, to ask me how great today was. For some reason I don't want to talk to Mom right now. I close the lid to my laptop, fast, and I run to the bathroom off the kitchen. I flush the toilet and run the water in the sink. Mom's voice will be cracking on the phone again. I just know it. Right now, I don't want to hear her voice cracking that way.

I'm not sure why. I just don't.

CHAPTER 8

McDonald's. That's the big surprise. We're going to McDonald's for dinner.

At school on Monday I'm going to ask Hannah if any of her babysitters ever took her and her little sister to McDonald's. So far Shelby hasn't done any of the things Hannah said. I haven't had any soda. She hasn't been texting any boyfriend on her phone, if she has one. And I definitely haven't been allowed to curse.

Will tells Shelby his order.

"A cheeseburger Happy Meal. Plain," he says. Then he says it again louder. "Plain."

Shelby laughs a little and says,

"Okay, Will. How about you tell them at the counter when we get there?"

I get that squeezing feeling in my stomach again.

"At the counter?" I say. "We usually go through the drive-thru and bring it home."

Will closes the lid of his laptop.

"I want to eat it there!" he says. "Eat it there, Mimi!"

I can feel Shelby looking at me. My face gets hot.

"Oh," she says, "I didn't think of that. Sure. If you want to bring it back here, that's fine."

"Eat it there!" Will says. "I want to eat it there!"

Right before she died, Gram took me to McDonald's. By myself. Just me and Gram. We sat in one of the little booths with only two seats. Gram had a coffee, and I had my usual Chicken McNuggets and fries. Gram opened up paper napkins on the table. We pretended we were having a picnic. We brought Will back a Happy Meal with a plain cheeseburger, just the way he liked. We didn't tell anyone that we went alone. Not even Mom. I knew Will would be upset if he found out we went because McDonald's is one of his favorite places. I felt a little sad about that.

"It's fine," I say. "We can eat there."

Shelby tells us to go brush our teeth before we go. I don't know why we have to do this since my teeth are only going to get dirty again from the McDonald's, but I do it anyway. Downstairs Shelby waits by the door with her car keys in her hand. Will and I put on our hoodies and zip them up. Shelby puts hers on too, but she leaves it open in the front. This is the first thing she's done all day that reminds me of Hannah's babysitters.

"You guys ready?" she says. Before we can answer she says, "I don't know about you, but I'm starving. I'm so hungry I could eat a horse."

We get into Shelby's little blue car. I buckle my seatbelt, but Will doesn't buckle his. Instead he looks down by his feet, out the side window and over at me. Shelby tells him to please buckle his seatbelt. I reach over and snap it in for him.

When we start driving, Will is very quiet.

"You okay, Will?" I say.

The sky is getting darker. I see the streetlights coming on outside Will's window as we drive.

"They don't have horses at McDonald's," he says. "No, they don't."

I look at Will sitting next to me. The streetlights make shadows on the side of his face.

"It's just an expression," I say.

He looks straight ahead and nods his head up and down, fast, three times.

"It's just an expression," he says.

CHAPTER 9

When we get there, it's crowded. There's hardly any place to stand with all the people waiting in line. Shelby says to stay close to her and holds Will's hand. I'm kind of surprised that he lets her. Right away Will starts getting nervous that we won't find a place to sit. He sticks the sleeve of his sweatshirt in his mouth and chews the edge.

"It's too crowded," he says. "Why is it too crowded?"

A little kid behind me steps on the back of my sneaker when we move forward. I have to twist my foot around to get my sneaker back on.

"It's too crowded," Will says again. "We'll never find a seat. Never."

Shelby stands on her tiptoes to try to look into the dining room.

"I have an idea," she says. She looks at me. "Why don't you guys go find us a seat while I wait for the food?"

She asks me what I want, and I tell her Chicken McNuggets and a small fries. Then I take Will by the sleeve— the one he isn't chewing on—and pull Will through the crowd to the dining room. The dining room is crowded, too. There are little kids everywhere. Will puts his hands over his ears.

"Oh, no," he says. "Oh, no! We'll never find a place to sit."

I look around the room for a seat. The tables are full of kids and parents and wrappers. I take a few steps forward so I can check for empty tables.

Will grabs my arm and squeezes. I'm thinking that I should tell Shelby we need to take the food home when Will takes off running toward an empty booth near the back. He runs past a woman in a pink jacket carrying a tray full of food and drinks. She lifts the tray just in time as Will zooms by.

"Excuse me!" she says in a loud voice.

She looks toward Will, but he's already in the back sitting at the booth. She gives me a nasty look, like it's my fault, and shakes her head.

I slide in the booth next to Will. The sleeve of his sweatshirt is wet. He puts it back in his mouth to chew, but I pull his arm down. He stops for a minute but then goes right back to chewing. I look around at all the tables to see if there's anyone I know from school. For a minute I think that the girl in a tie-dye shirt a few tables away might be from my homeroom. I grab Will's arm and hold it down to keep him from chewing on his sleeve. When she turns to talk to the girl next to her, I see it isn't her after all. I let go of his arm and let him chew.

Just then I spot Shelby coming through the crowd with the tray. It's hard to miss her red hair. She looks around for us. Will jumps in his seat and calls her name.

She puts the tray down and hands Will his Happy Meal. Will starts to rip open the top of the red box, but she stops him.

"Do you do that at school, Will?" she says. "Or do you wait for everybody to get their food?"

Will stops and puts his hands on the table.

"Don't run in the hallway," he says. But then Shelby tells him to look at her, and he says, "Wait till everybody gets their food."

I don't love McDonald's as much as Will does, but the food does smell good. Shelby hands us napkins and straws. Will stares at his Happy Meal box like he's about to start drooling. Shelby looks at me and winks.

"All right, Will," she says. "Ready, set . . ."

Before she can finish, Will says, "Go," and opens the box. Shelby laughs. I do too. I take the first bite of my fries and taste the salt on my tongue.

I'm taking a sip of my fruit punch when it happens. Will drops a big blob of cheeseburger out of his mouth. It lands with a splat on the tray. He starts spitting. He sticks out his tongue and wipes it with his napkin.

"Oh, no! Oh, no!" he yells.

Shelby asks what's wrong, but now Will is crying and trying to wipe his tongue with more napkins. He keeps spitting on the tray. I close the yellow box of McNuggets because I'm not hungry anymore. I try not to look at the hunk of cheeseburger lying there on the tray. The girl in the tie-dye is staring at us. I can tell she's saying something about Will to the girl next to her by the way she looks at me. Will crumples a napkin and shoves it in his mouth. He swallows a piece of napkin and cries and cries.

"What is it, Will? What's wrong?" Shelby says.

Shelby takes the napkin out of his mouth, so he can't swallow any more of it. He stands up and bangs on the table. He keeps crying and screaming. I see the lady with the pink jacket and the tray looking at us. I feel my back sliding down the plastic booth. If I could slide all the way down to the floor, I would.

Shelby reaches over and peels open Will's cheeseburger. Will screams and points at the pickles and onions on top of the cheese.

"Okay, Will, okay," she says. "It's okay. We'll get you a new one."

"You'll get me a new one!" Will says. He wipes his nose on his sleeve. "You'll get me a new one! Yup!"

Shelby leans forward and takes Will's hands in hers, so he stops ripping the napkins. The lady with the pink jacket is sucking on her straw and looking at Will. He's still crying. Shelby tells him to take deep breaths to try to calm him down.

"Watch, Will, like me," she says. She breathes in through her nose and then blows a big breath that ruffles the napkins. "Smell the flowers," she says, and sniffs, "and blow out the candles," with another big breath.

The lady with the pink jacket sees me looking then. I sit up straight and stare right back at her. I look over at Will sniffing the air up his nose and then blowing the napkins and then back at the lady. She sips at her drink again, and then snaps her head forward when she sees me looking at her. I wish Will had knocked over her tray. I picture it in my mind, all of her food falling on the floor and a big cup of soda splattering her pink jacket.

Shelby gathers up all of the napkins Will ripped up and our wrappers and cups and shoves them all on the tray. She tells Will to put on his hoodie and zip it up. I zip mine too, even though Shelby doesn't tell me to.

When we get up to leave, I see the lady in the pink jacket looking at us again. Mom always says that people who look at Will aren't doing it to be mean. She says that they don't understand what is happening and that I should ignore them. I try to ignore the lady, but I just can't.

Shelby sees me looking at the lady and asks me if everything is okay. I just nod and stuff my hands in my pockets. Shelby puts her arm around Will. Just before we pass, she winks at me and then looks right at the lady.

"Nothing to see here," she says, raising her voice. "Show's over now."

At the counter Shelby orders a new cheeseburger for Will and Chicken McNuggets for me. Will says he wants extra french fries, so she orders two orders of those too. I'm not very hungry anymore, but I don't say anything to Shelby. Before we leave, Shelby opens up the Happy Meal right at the counter and peels open the bun to make sure it's plain.

"See that, Will?" she says, and Will says, "Yup," and nods really fast.

As Shelby opens the door, Will turns back to the counter and yells out, "Ladies can't start fights, but they can finish them!"

In the car as we buckle in, Shelby looks at me in the rearview mirror.

"Okay, wait, don't tell me," she says. "I think I know where that one's from. *The Aristocats*. Am I right?'"

I just nod. She smiles at me and then turns around. The backseat is dark as we pull away from McDonald's and onto the road. My stomach finally stops squeezing.

CHAPTER 10

At home Will says his cheeseburger is too cold. Gram used to say that Will was like Goldilocks because he always said his food was either too hot or too cold. We sit at the table while Shelby microwaves Will's cheeseburger. Will shoves his french fries into his mouth two or three at a time. I take little nibbles of the McNuggets. Mine aren't hot, either, but I don't say anything to Shelby.

When Shelby sits down, she asks me if my McNuggets are okay. I just nod and take some more little bites.

"Not hungry anymore?" she says.

She says it quietly and gives me this half smile.

"That's fine," she says. "You don't have to finish if you don't want to."

I just nod and close the box. Then I get up and throw the box in the garbage. In the bathroom I wash my hands and look in the mirror. My face is red. I splash some water on it and wipe my face with the towel. I think about Will yelling at McDonald's and the people staring, especially that lady with the pink jacket. I think about Shelby saying the show was over loud enough for everyone to hear. My throat feels tight. But I'm not mad anymore.

When I come out of the bathroom, Will is crumpling up the wrappers. I knew he wouldn't eat the extra order of fries he said he wanted. Dad says that one of Will's favorite pastimes is throwing out food. Will loves Oreos, but he'll only eat the kind that come in the little packages of six. If you give him six Oreos out of the regular family pack, he'll take one bite and then throw the rest in the garbage. It doesn't matter how many times you tell him they're the same exact kind.

Shelby gathers up all the wrappers from the table and throws them away.

"I guess your eyes are bigger than your belly, huh, Will?" Shelby says.

She takes the trash bag outside to the can in the driveway that Dad showed her before they left. I ask Will if he wants to play *Minecraft* again. He doesn't answer me.

"Will," I say, "do you want to play or not?"

I tell him that we'll probably have to go to bed soon. Usually that gets him to listen when he's not paying attention. But he just sits there looking down. He lifts his shirt up to expose his belly button and stares at it. Shelby comes back in then and asks him what's wrong.

"My belly is flat," he says, "and my eyes are small and round."

"Yes," Shelby says. "I guess they are."

She raises her eyebrows and looks at me. I can tell she doesn't get it. He's trying to tell her that there's no way his eyes are bigger than his belly.

"It's just an expression," I tell him.

He nods and opens his laptop.

"It's just an expression," he says.

CHAPTER 11

We're upstairs brushing our teeth to get ready for bed when Mom calls. Will comes into the bathroom with me while I'm brushing my teeth. Usually I'd tell him to get out and that I need privacy, but tonight I let him come in. When I'm done I stand there and watch him put the toothpaste on his dry toothbrush. I tell him that he needs to wet his brush, but he doesn't listen. He doesn't like his toothbrush to be wet. I don't know why. I don't tell him to wet it again.

On the way downstairs I hear Shelby talking to Mom. I hear Shelby say, "a little upset" and "McDonald's" and "wrong order." She doesn't say "freak out" or "meltdown." When I come into the living room, Shelby hands me the phone. My stomach squeezes.

"Oh, honey," Mom says, "Did he have a meltdown? Is that what happened?"

I think about the last time Will had a meltdown. It was last year at Target, and Will wanted *Minecraft* figures. Mom said he already had those. Will took the box and threw it on the floor. When Mom tried to drag him out, he dropped down on the floor and started screaming and kicking. I tried to help pull him up, but he screamed even harder. The manager came over and asked Mom if she needed help. I stood behind Mom and stared down at the floor. Mom had to call Dad to come help her get Will off the floor. We haven't gone back to Target since then.

"No," I tell Mom on the phone, "he just got upset about his order."

I tell her about the cheeseburger and the pickles and onions. I don't tell her about the lady staring at us. I do tell her what Will yelled out on the way out of McDonald's because I know that will make Mom laugh. It does.

"So, it sounds like Shelby handled it," she says, and I say yes. After all, Will didn't end up on the floor.

She asks to talk to Will. When I give him the phone, he yells into the phone, "You're only in trouble if you get caught," and then hands the phone back to me. Mom's voice cracks a little when she says good night and that she'll see me in the morning.

"That one's from *Aladdin*," I tell Shelby after I hang up.

Upstairs Shelby tells Will that she'll be putting him to bed tonight and that she'll read him as many stories as he wants. I can hear him asking for Mom when I pass by his room.

"I want Mom to read to me," he says. "I want Mom to read my stories."

I stop in the doorway to his room. He has on his *Minecraft* pajamas and his *Minecraft* pillowcases and his *Minecraft* comforter. Shelby sits on the edge of his bed in a T-shirt with hearts on it and plaid pajama pants. When I see Hannah at school on Monday, I'm going to ask her if she's ever seen any of her babysitters in pajamas.

"Will," I say. "Mom will be home tomorrow. She'll read to you tomorrow night. She can't read to you now."

He nods and says, "Yup," and wipes his eyes with his pajama top.

The night that Gram died, Mom came home and sat Will and me on the couch to tell us. She said that Gram went to be with God and that she wasn't in any pain. She kept saying that Gram passed away. I remember that even though I felt really sad, I could tell that Will didn't understand. He kept kicking the couch and not looking at Mom.

"Mom," I said as he kept kicking the couch, "you're going to have to say 'died.'"

Mom nodded and said very quietly, "Gram died."

Will stopped kicking the couch then and said, "Gram died?"

"Yes, Will," Mom said. "Gram died."

Then he pulled up his shirt to wipe his eyes.

I say good night and head toward my room. I pull my purple comforter all the way up to my chin and close my eyes. For some reason I feel like if I open them, Gram will be standing there looking down at me. I don't know why I think that. I just do.

*　*　*　*　*

When I open my eyes again, it's not Gram standing there. It's Shelby. Will can't sleep. Neither can I. Shelby says she has an idea.

"Do you guys have sleeping bags?" she says. "Let's have a slumber party."

Will is waiting outside my room. We go downstairs to the coat closet where Mom keeps the sleeping bags. Will's is an old one with Thomas the Tank Engine on it. I hand it to him and take my red one and give Shelby the extra one we have that's navy blue and covered with stars.

"Thomas is for babies," Will says. He shoves the sleeping bag at me. "Yes, it is."

Just then my stomach squeezes because I am way too tired for Will to freak out again. Shelby reaches for the Thomas bag and gives Will the other one with stars.

"I'll sleep with Thomas," Shelby says. "I don't mind being a baby."

We start laying the sleeping bags on the living room rug when Shelby says she has an idea. She motions for me to follow her to the kitchen.

"A lot of kids in my class love to be in tents," she says. "Let's make Will a tent."

I remember that Gram used to make Will what she called a quiet spot at her house. She used an old table and hung blankets over the sides. Will would get underneath and watch his videos on his iPad. As we pull the chairs into the living room to make Will's tent, I realize that I almost forgot all about the quiet space. Until now.

Shelby arranges the chairs in a square then hangs a bunch of blankets we found in the closet. She lays out Will's sleeping bag underneath.

"Like at Gram's house," he says. "Like at Gram's house, Mimi."

"Yup," I say. "Just like at Gram's house."

Shelby holds the blanket up for Will to go under.

"Ready?" Shelby says, and Will nods. She pulls the blanket down and says, "Good night, Will."

I get into my sleeping bag and zip

up the side. Shelby squirms into the Thomas sleeping bag. I think about that imaginary babysitting factory and wonder if any of Hannah's babysitters ever slept in a Thomas sleeping bag. With her red hair sticking out, Shelby looks a little silly in that sleeping bag. I look over at the tent she made with Will underneath.

"Sleep tight," he says. "Don't let the bed bugs bite."

I try to think what movie that's from, but then I realize it isn't from a movie. It's what Gram used to say when she put us to bed.

"It's just an expression," he says.

Shelby and I both start laughing.

*   *   *   *   *

A little later, after Will falls asleep, I ask Shelby about her class. She says that the kids are all different. One kid lies on the floor sometimes and looks up at the ceiling fan. Another kid likes to open and close the door so much that they have to keep it locked. Another kid can name the capitals of every state and the names of every president we've ever had. Another kid hardly talks but can sing the lyrics to every Beatles song you can think of.

She tells me that she has a cousin with a disability. Sometimes Mom uses that word when she talks about Will. Shelby says her cousin is in a wheelchair, the kind with a big tray in front.

She has cerebral palsy and has to use a device to speak.

"The way the woman at McDonald's was looking at Will," she says, "is the way people look at my cousin all the time."

She says her cousin is the reason she is studying to be a Special Ed teacher. She says her cousin is very funny and makes jokes all the time on her device.

"Will's pretty funny, too," I say, because he is.

"Yes, he is," Shelby says. "Will is very lucky to have a sister like you."

Mom and Dad say that to me all the time. For some reason, though, it feels different when Shelby says it.

I look over at Will's tent. I smile to myself in the dark, even though no one can see me.

CHAPTER 12

In the morning we clean up the sleeping bags. I help Shelby put all the chairs back in the kitchen. Mom calls to say that they'll be home soon. She says that Will can wait for her to have his toast if he wants, Shelby says.

"What do you think, Will?" Shelby says. "Do you want to wait for Mom, or do you want me to make your toast?"

Will is already at the table playing *Minecraft*. I sit down at the table and open my laptop so we can play together. He doesn't look up from his laptop.

"Will," I say, "Shelby asked you a

question. Do you want her to make your toast?"

Will looks up at me and then at Shelby.

"You can make my toast," he says. "You can make it."

Shelby and I look at each other. She gives me a big thumbs-up.

Shelby checks the visual schedule on the wall.

"Tan, but not too brown," Shelby says. "Coming right up."

Will blows up my crops. I plant new ones.

"What about you, Mia?" Shelby says. "Do you like yours tan too?"

Will looks up at me. I know that he likes it when we like the same things. I don't know how I know this. I just do.

"I like mine tan, too," I say. "Same as Will's."

Shelby leans down to watch the toast in the toaster oven. She pulls out the pieces and brings them over on a plate.

"How did I do, Will?" she asks. "Is that tan enough?"

I look over at the plate of toast. It is definitely tan.

Will grabs a piece and holds it up to examine it.

"Remember," he says. "Fish are friends, not food."

Then he takes a big bite.

"That's from *Finding Nemo*" I say,

as I take a piece of toast and put it on my plate. "It means he likes it."

Shelby sits down with us at the table. I look at Will and then at Shelby. I think about Hannah and all of her babysitters. We're just like any other kids sitting at the table with their babysitter, eating toast that is tan but not too tan. Just the way we like it.

Vocabulary List

autism: A condition that affects someone's abilities in relating to and communicating with other people. Also known as Autism Spectrum Disorder or ASD.

cerebral palsy: A kind of disability that affects a person's muscles and the ability to move.

conveyor belt: A moving strip that transports objects from one place to another.

disability: A problem that can make it difficult or impossible for a person to see, speak, hear, move around, or learn.

echolalia: Repeating word for word what another person is saying.

empathy: The ability to feel and understand what other people are feeling.

expression: A popular group of words that means something that is different from what the words say. For example, "to kick the bucket" means "to die."

interpreter: Someone who can explain in language what someone is saying.

literal mind: A mind who doesn't understand figures of speech. For example, if you say to someone with a literal mind that it was "raining cats and dogs," they would imagine cats and dogs falling from the sky.

on the spectrum: A term used to describe people with forms of autism.

sensory gym: A place where kids with autism can bounce, spin, jump, and do other things that help them to feel calm.

Social Story: A story used to help people with autism understand language and situations that are difficult for them to comprehend.

social studies: A class or course that studies society and how it works.

Special Ed: An educational program for students with learning or other disabilities.

CPSIA information can be obtained
at www.ICGtesting.com
Printed in the USA
LVHW091448210419
614986LV00001B/1/P